To **Alice**

For being good.
MERRY CHRISTMAS!

From

It was a crisp Christmas Eve
and Santa and his reindeers
were busy delivering presents to
all the good boys and girls.

Santa's sleigh zoomed over houses, twisting
and turning silently through the snowy night sky.
Santa squeezed down and up and up and down
chimneys, carefully and quietly delivering
lots of presents.

4

ll was going to plan until he reached the second to last ouse on his list.

Suddenly, Santa noticed one of the presents was missing!

The reindeer looked in Santa's sack, they searched everywhere but the present was nowhere to be found! "Oh no!" exclaimed Santa. "It must have fallen off the sleigh!"

5

Santa wondered what to do.
He had no time to look for the present
but he didn't want to disappoint anyone
on his Christmas list.

Then
Santa had a
FANTASTIC
idea!

Naughty & Nice LIST

He looked at his delivery map to see where they were.
Then he checked his list to see who had been naughty or ni

At the very
top of the list was **Alice**.
So Santa and Blitzen (the smallest of
all the reindeer) squeezed
down the chimney...

7

her

into

quietly

crept

...and

bedroom.

Alice yawned, stretched and rubbed her eyes. She thought she was still **dreaming** until Blitzen licked her face with his long, wet, pink tongue - YUCK!

"I need your help!" boomed Santa.
He explained that a present had
fallen off the sleigh and
Santa wanted **Alice**
to go with Blitzen
to find it.

Alice of course was **VERY** happy to help.

9

It was cold and snowy outside so **Alice** put on her warmest hat and long, stripy scarf.

Alice and Blitzen looked through Santa's telescope.

They looked down past the houses and through the trees, trying to find the lost present.

Suddenly they spotted it, sitting on top of a pile of snow at the bottom of a big hill.

She jumped on Blitzen's back and gave him a friendly pat and little tickle behind his fluffy ears. Then with a gentle nudge they flew high into the starry night sky.

Up and up they soared

and higher
higher

until Blitzen did a
loop the loop,
a flip and a flop
and landed with a bop
next to the pile of snow...

but the present had gon

12

Alice and Blitzen looked around but couldn't see the present anywhere!

All of a sudden Blitzen's wet nose began to twitch and itch and wibble and wobble. What had he found?

Alice saw a bright orange carrot sticking out of the snow. "Who likes carrots?" she wondered. Perhaps this was a clue to where the present had gone.

13

Then they saw a tiny white and grey bunny rabbit.

"Hello Mrs Rabbit, we're looking for a missing gift which fell from Santa's sleigh. Have you seen anything?"

The bunny twitched her nose, rubbed her ears and pointed a fluffy white paw at a line of acorns.

14

"Who likes acorns?"
wondered **Alice**.

Then looking down, they noticed a
bouncy red squirrel staring back at them.
They followed him, picking up the **acorns** one by one,
not knowing who or what would be at the end of the trail.

15

As they picked up the final acorn, they noticed a nose-less, button-less, very sad snowman right in front of them.

His carrot nose had fallen off and his acorn buttons had been lost but there, poking out from under his black hat, was a shiny Christmas present!

16

Hurray, they had found the present...
but why did the snowman have it?

The sad snowman explained that
every year he felt forgotten as
he never received a present.
When he found this one he was so
happy. However, now he knew
it belonged to someone
else, he wanted to
give it back.

17

Feeling sorry for the snowman,
Alice decided to help.
She placed the half-eaten **carrot**
on the snowman's face for his nose
and the **acorn** buttons on his body –
but the snowman still looked sad.

Then **Alice**
had a brilliant idea!

18

She undid her fluffy scarf and tied it around the surprised snowman.

Then she replaced the snowman's old black hat with her warm knitted one.

The snowman was so happy! At last he had his very OWN Christmas present!

Alice and Blitzen flew as fast as they could to get the missing present back in time for Christmas morning.

Back at home Alice gave Blitzen a big hug, then watched as her new friend flew up into the sky and home to Santa.

Alice placed the gift under the tree with a huge sigh of relief!

When **Alice** woke up on Christmas morning, she wondered if it had all been a dream. Then she looked out of her window...

...and there in the distance was the happy snowman waving at her and he was still wearing his lovely Christmas present.

The end